# Savage PRINCESS

CHERI MARIE

Book Cover Designed by: Tiffany Black, T.E. Black Designs

Photographer: Jean Maureen Woodfin, JW Photography and Covers

Models: Kyle English and Katy McCain

Editor: Courtney Lynn Rose, Full Bloom Editorial Services

Formatted by: Brenda Wright, Formatting Done Wright

# Dedication

To my girls, who took a chance on me when I decided to host my first anthology…

JM Schalm, LB Russell, Brandy Dorsch, Reagan Hollow, Carissa Laryea, Ava Harper Kent, Barb Shuler, Jaime Russell, Ava Danielle, Bethany Loughlin-Frost, & Kelsey Jensen

Thank you <3

# Table of Contents

# Prologue

"Do you want me to expose you for what you've done? I'm sure your daughter wouldn't be pleased, let alone the police department."

Raised voices come from my father's office. I listen silently, though I know I shouldn't.

"Fine." My father sighs, exasperated. "I'll do whatever you want."

"My time as Mayor is coming to an end. When it does, Ethan will be running for Mayor of this town. When he wins, he wants your daughter's hand."

I'm horrified. I despise Ethan Franklyn. He walks around like people should worship him because his father is the Mayor. Most of the girls we went to school with fall at his feet and think he's a modern-day Adonis, but not me. His arrogant attitude and air of self-entitlement is a total turn off.

Emilio Manzini, now he's a modern-day Adonis. Tall, muscular, beautiful bronzed skin, brown hair, dark brown eyes, and a smile that's sweet yet savage. I scoff at myself. If my father knew I was daydreaming about the son of his nemesis… he'd blow a gasket, or have me committed.

"No! I won't do that. Fallyn was never part of the deal, and she's *not* a bargaining chip."

I've heard enough. Making my way down the hallway, I push the door open to find my father and the Mayor standing in front of his desk. The Mayor obviously trying to use intimidation tactics on my father.

"Everything okay, Daddy?"

"Everything is fine, Fallyn. We were just having a discussion. Go downstairs and I'll be down to cook us dinner in a minute."

"Okay."

Slowly, I close the door behind me and make my way back down the hallway, and down the stairs to put on a movie while I wait. No matter what I do though, I can't get into the movie after what I overheard. My father wouldn't really agree with something like that, right? Besides, we're in the 21st century, arranged marriages are seriously outdated.

Lost in my thoughts, I'm startled when my dad and the Mayor come down the stairs.

"It was good to see you, Fallyn."

"You too, Mr. Mayor. Have a good night."

He nods, shakes my father's hand, and then disappears out the door. Standing up from the couch, I follow my father into the kitchen and pour myself a glass of sweet tea.

"So, what was that all about? It sounded pretty intense."

"It's nothing you need to worry about." He places a kiss on my forehead, completely dismissing my questioning eyes as he moves around the kitchen to make dinner.

"Dad, we're a team, remember? If something is going on, you can tell me. I'm not a little girl anymore. I can handle it."

"As I said, it's nothing you have to worry about, princess."

"Okay." I raise my hands in surrender. Obviously, he's not going to tell me what they were arguing about. Letting the subject drop, for now, I ask, "So what are we having for dinner?"

"Steak, potatoes, and veggies."

"Mmm... sounds delicious! Can I help?"

"Sure, you can cut up the potatoes and get them ready for the oven."

"Okay." I grab the potatoes, a pan, and the cutting board. "Remember the first time mom let me help her cook?"

"How could I forget? You turned the mixer on without it being all the way in the bowl and mashed potatoes went all over the kitchen."

We both burst into a fit of laughter while we continue to work on finishing up dinner.

"I miss her."

"Me too, princess."

"Has there been any luck finding the driver who hit her?"

He's silent for a moment. "Not yet, but we'll find them. I'm sure of it."

I smile fondly at the memory of my amazing mother. She was killed in a car crash a year ago, and I miss her more every day. My father quickly changes the subject while we eat and talk, as if the conversation I'd overheard hadn't upset him, or ticked me off. After finishing up, I clean up the dishes and put them away.

The rest of the night we continue to reminisce about all the funny things that happened while I was growing up. It's crazy to think how long ago some of it was, yet I remember like it was yesterday. "I think I'm going to go to bed, I'm tired and I have to go shopping tomorrow."

"Okay, princess, goodnight."

My dad stands, kissing me on the forehead before we both head to bed.

My first shift at Manzini's is Friday, and I need to shop for some new clothes. Grabbing my keys, I head for the mall. I personally despise the mall but I don't really want to drive an extra 45 minutes out of town to my favorite store.

When I pull in, I immediately notice Ethan Franklyn's car in the parking lot. Great. I quickly park and hop out, wanting to get this over with and hoping to successfully avoid Ethan.

An older gentleman holds the door for me at one of the many entrances and I thank him graciously. I scan the food court and don't see Ethan anywhere in sight; thank God. Just when I think I'm going to successfully make it in and out of here without running into that arrogant ass, I turn the corner and run smack into him.

"Well, hello there, Fallyn." His cocky smirk makes my skin crawl as I quickly step away from him.

"Hi, Ethan," my tone clearly unimpressed.

His blue eyes narrow as he runs them up and down my body. His usual sandy brown curls are cut short, and he's dressed like he's going to a fancy dinner instead of wandering the mall like a creepy little mall rat. His broad shoulders fill up his Oxford shirt that is tucked into a pair of black slacks. If he wasn't such an asshole, he might be slightly attractive.

"When are you going to let me take you out?"

"How about never? Goodbye, Ethan." I take a step to get past him but he blocks my way.

"Come on, Fallyn, I know you want me."

"Goodbye, Ethan," I repeat, again trying to make my way around him.

He blocks me again so I move to the other side but he snatches my arm.

"Let me go, Ethan!"

"You will be mine, it's only a matter of time," he sneers, stepping in closer and leaning towards my ear.

Someone clears their throat and Ethan immediately releases my arm after looking over my shoulder. I spin around to find Emilio Manzini standing behind me, glaring at Ethan.

"Emilio. Hi."

Suddenly breathless from our close proximity, I take a step back—but to the side so I'm not backed up to Ethan. Emilio glances down at me and smiles, but quickly turns his attention back to Ethan.

"Is there a problem here?" his voice is deep and all business. I try my hardest to suppress the shudder that threatens to roll over my body as his voice hits my ears.

"Nope, no problem here," Ethan replies through gritted teeth, anger coloring his words.

"Good. Now leave and if I ever see you grab Fallyn like you just did, I'll break your fucking arm. Do you understand me?"

"Yea, sure Emilio… see you around, Fallyn."

Ethan disappears into the crowded food court and I breathe a sigh of relief.

"You okay?"

I turn back to Emilio. His sinfully sexy brown eyes meet mine, genuine concern written on his face. I smile shyly at him.

"Yea, I'm okay."

"Good." He smiles at me again, showing off those dimples that make me melt.

"Well, I should go get my shopping done so I can get out of here as soon as possible."

"Sure. Do you mind if I walk with you? Just in case Ethan comes back."

Does Emilio really want to shop with me? I try to hide the excited nervousness bubbling up inside of me, and reply with a nonchalant, "Sure."

We walk side-by-side through the mall, talking, and every once in a while our hands brush against each other. The feeling doesn't go unnoticed but neither of us says anything.

"So, what're you shopping for?"

"Some clothes for my new job."

"That's great! Where?"

"Your uncle's place."

Emilio's steps halt and his brows crease. "Are you sure that's such a good idea?"

"Why not?"

"Maybe the obvious? You're the chief's daughter, working in a bar my uncle owns and my family frequents. Not exactly the best place for you to be working, don't you think?"

"I'll be fine. Your uncle isn't going to let anything happen to me."

"I just think it's dangerous for you to work there," he pushes.

"I'm not worried. I can take care of myself," I say, my temper starting to rise. Dimples and dreamy eyes aside, who the hell does he think he is, trying to tell me where I should and shouldn't work?

He sighs, exasperated. "Fine. But you have to promise me, if you feel the slightest bit unsafe, you will call me immediately… Promise me, Fallyn."

"Okay, I promise," I agree quickly, eager to end this conversation.

Emilio hangs with me while I continue to shop. After multiple stores, I have one last stop. Victoria Secret. We stop at the entrance and I glance at Emilio.

"I can totally help in this store." That sexy smirk spreads across his face.

I side eye him. "I think not."

He laughs, putting his hands up in surrender. "Fine. I will wait right here," he says as he takes a seat in the massage chair just outside the store. "But if you change your mind, all you have to do is ask."

He winks and I roll my eyes as I turn on my heel and head into the store quickly, hoping to hide the blush creeping up my neck to my cheeks.

When I'm done, he insists on walking me to my car. Pulling the keys from my pocket, I hit the key fob to unlock the doors.

"You really didn't have to stay with me. I can handle Ethan." We're standing next to my open door, but I don't want to get in yet. I want to prolong this moment for just a few more precious seconds if I can.

"I know, but I wanted to stay."

Emilio reaches out and takes my hand, lightly running his thumb over my knuckles. The contact sends shivers through me. He leans in and, just as I think he's about to kiss me, his phone rings. I silently curse it under my breath. He pulls back and checks the caller ID before slipping it back into his pocket.

"I'm sorry, I have to go."

"Okay."

I'm disappointed but smile sweetly at him. He leans in, placing a soft, sweet kiss to my cheek.

"Bye, Fallyn," he whispers as he pulls back.

"Bye, Emilio," I breathe out.

He walks away, and I take a moment to appreciate the view. Sliding into the driver's seat of my car, my hand goes to my cheek where his lips were. Sighing, I start my car and take off towards home, completely confused as to what today was all about.

# Chapter 1

## *Three Years Later*

### Fallyn

"Fallyn, honey, can I talk to you for a minute?" my dad asks as he stands in the doorway of my room.

"Sure, Dad, just let me finish getting ready for work."

"Okay, I'll be in my office," he says as he turns and heads down the hallway.

I finish putting on my makeup and slip my feet into my boots. Grabbing my jacket and keys off my bed, I practically jog down the hall to my dad's office.

Knocking first, I push open the door and walk in, taking a seat in the chair on the opposite side of his desk.

"So, what did you want to talk to me about?"

He takes a deep breath and stares at me blankly for a moment like he's trying to collect his thoughts.

"You know I love you, right?" he says, pausing.

Raising an eyebrow at him, I answer, "Of course, Daddy."

"You know I only want what's best for you…"

"I know, Dad. Can you please just get to the point? I have to get to work."

He rolls his eyes. "You know Mayor Franklyn's father was a dear friend of mine… Well, I had lunch with the Mayor the other day. He's a nice, wealthy, steady young man. Can you believe he isn't married?"

Immediately, there's a nauseous feeling in the pit of my stomach. He wouldn't. My mind flashes back to the conversation I overheard between my father and Ethan's father three years ago. *If Ethan wins Mayor, he wants your daughter's hand.* I feel like I'm going to vomit, and I just need him to say what he has to say so I can go.

"Dad, you're babbling and not making any damn sense. Get to the point or I'm leaving."

He closes his eyes for a moment before he speaks again. "He asked for your hand in marriage. I gave him my blessing."

I stare blankly at him before pure rage takes over and I spring to my feet. "YOU WHAT! You do realize we're in the 21st century, where women have the choice to marry who they want, right?"

"But Fallyn… I…"

"NO!" I stand and pace my father's office. "I overheard your conversation with his father, in your office that night. What the hell ever happened to the whole *'Fallyn is not a bargaining chip'* thing? Never in my life did I think you would actually agree to something like that!"

"Fallyn, honey, I'm sorry, I—"

"I don't care what you told him, it isn't happening. Ethan Franklyn is a vile, self-absorbed, egotistical prick. I will *not* marry a man like that! You know what, I have to go."

Grabbing my things, I storm out of his office and out of the house, slamming the door behind me.

I slide into the seat of my SUV and head towards Manzini Lounge and Nightclub. Pulling into the lot designated for employees, I park my car, grab my things, and make my way inside to get the place ready for business.

As I approach the back door, a hand covers my mouth and a strong arm wraps around my waist. I start to struggle and fight back until a voice as smooth as whiskey is in my ear.

"*Bellissima*, you should really be more careful in this neighborhood. Some big, tatted, muscular Italian guy could snatch you up."

Grabbing his hand, I remove it from my mouth. "I would advise them against that decision. See, I already have a sexy, tall, muscular, badass Italian boyfriend, and I'm sure he wouldn't take too kindly to another man touching his goodies," I say as I spin in his arms.

"I'd kill him," he says without cracking a smile. From his tone, there is no doubt in my mind that he would kill someone for touching me, without a second thought.

Emilio Manzini is the epitome of everything sexy and dangerous, wrapped up in a perfectly defined muscular package, tied with a bow. Not to mention, he's my boss' nephew, and the son of Eli Manzini, the Italian mob boss my father is trying to take down.

Standing on my toes, I run my fingers through his dark locks and place my lips on his. He grabs the back of my head, entangling his fingers in my hair, as he holds me in place and deepens the kiss. His other hand runs down my back to cup my ass.

"Mmm… I've missed you so much," he whispers against my lips.

"I've missed you, too."

A sexy smirk plays on his lips, "Why don't you show me how much you've missed me."

"Your uncle will be here soon; do you want to get caught?"

He raises an eyebrow at me. "To be honest, I couldn't give a shit."

I look around for a sign that anyone is pulling in. When I don't see anyone, I grab Emilio by the hand and lead him to the storage building. Pulling my keys out of my pocket, I quickly unlock the door and we slip inside, relocking it behind us.

I spin around and Emilio is already undressed, standing naked, in all his glory. Quickly stripping myself of my clothes, I barely have a chance to step out of my jeans before he grabs me by my ass. I instinctively wrap my legs around him as he lifts me, pressing me against the wall. His lips crush mine in a deep, passionate kiss that's full of need. His growing erection presses against my now heated pussy.

"Emilio," I moan. "I need you."

Hanging onto me with one arm, he uses his other to reach between us and center himself at my opening. With a quick thrust, he fills me and we both moan in unison. Placing both his hands on my hips, I link my arms around his neck and he falls into a delicious rhythm.

I meet his every thrust as he plows into me. His lips move from mine as he places kisses down my neck, lightly nipping at the skin. My orgasm builds as he picks up his pace.

"I'm going to come," I gasp.

I tighten my legs around him, pulling him closer, forcing him deeper inside me. I dig my nails into his back as my legs start to tremble. He continues his assault, as I come undone around him, screaming out his name.

After a few more thrusts, he grunts and lightly bites the flesh of my shoulder as he explodes inside me. He clings to me as he slowly lowers us to the floor, leaving me straddling his lap.

"What are you doing to me?" he whispers, resting his forehead against mine. "You know if anyone finds out about us, all hell is going to break loose. But I just can't stay away from you. I'm drawn to you like I've never been drawn to anyone before. I should stay away, but I don't think I can. I don't want to."

"My father would shit bricks if he knew I was seeing Manzini's son. For Christ sakes, he wants me to marry Mayor Franklyn."

Emilio chuckles for a moment before all traces of amusement leave his face. "Wait, what?"

"Yea. He called me into his office at home before I left for work to tell me Ethan asked for my hand in marriage, and my father gave his blessing."

"Are you fucking serious?" Emilio is enraged and moves to lift us from the ground but I stop him.

"Babe, calm down. I told him there is no way in hell I would marry Ethan Franklyn." Placing my hand on his cheek, I turn his face to look at mine. "There is no one that could ever come between us. Not my father, not your father, and sure as hell not Ethan Franklyn."

Leaning in, I place a kiss on his lips and carefully ease myself off him. Before I can walk away to gather my clothes, he grabs my hand to stop me. Reaching over to grab his t-shirt, he softly wipes it over my pussy and the inside of my thighs, removing the evidence of our lovemaking.

"Okay, all clean," he says, giving me a slap on the ass as I walk away to gather my clothes and get dressed. Using his shirt, he wipes himself off too before sliding his pants on. He stands, kisses me, and straightens my just fucked hair before unlocking the door. We're unaware anyone else is here until his uncle's voice echoes through the parking lot.

"What the hell were you two doing in there?"

"Oh, hi Alex. He was just helping me look for some extra pool sticks since a few got broken during that bar fight last week. We couldn't find any though."

"Oh okay, well everything is pretty much ready for opening. I just need you to slice some limes and oranges."

"Okay, I'll get right on it." I turn back to Emilio, "Thanks for helping me look for the pool sticks," I say with a wink.

"Anytime."

Alex glances between us but he doesn't say anything. Waving goodbye to Emilio, I head into the bar to finish the prep work.

# Chapter 2

## Fallyn

The club is packed, and one of our bartenders just walked out; this is not what I need tonight. People are getting antsy, and Alex is coming my way.

"What the hell is the hold-up, Fallyn? Where's Alecia?"

"She just quit and walked out. I'm trying to keep up but it's damn near impossible with all these people."

He runs his hands over his face, exasperated. "Call Emilio and ask him to come in and help for a couple hours."

"I don't have his number." Alex just side eyes me, giving me that '*do I look like an idiot to you*' look.

I throw my hands up. "Okay, okay. I'll call him."

I pull my phone out of my pocket and click on his name. It rings twice before he picks up.

"Hello, *mia Regina.* I thought you were working until close?"

"I am. Your uncle told me to call you. Alecia walked out so it's just me. Can you come help for a couple hours?"

"Sure, *Bellissima.* I'll be there soon."

"Thank you." I blow a quick kiss through the phone and slip it back into my pocket.

I take three drink orders and start serving them up when I feel eyes on me. I try not to pay it any mind but the intensity is overwhelming. When I finally give in to the urge to look for the burning eyes, I spot Ethan at the end of the bar. Fuck. Not tonight, and definitely not when Emilio is on his way here.

I finish serving up the drinks I was working on and cash them out before I make my way to Ethan.

"Good evening, Mayor. What can I get for you?"

"There's no need for formalities, Fallyn. Especially not when you're going to be my wife."

I chuckle at the notion that he really thinks this is going to happen. He stands and pulls me around the end of the bar, attempting to lean in and kiss me. I place my hands on his chest and try to push him away, struggling against him, knowing Emilio will be here any second and this won't end well.

Just then, I look over Ethan's shoulder at Emilio bounding towards us, his eyes alight with renewed rage—shit is about to hit the fan. Emilio snatches Ethan's hands from my waist and steps between us.

"What the fuck do you think you're doing?" Emilio growls at Ethan.

"Just showing my future wife some affection," he says smugly.

Emilio steps close to Ethan, almost nose-to-nose and close enough that only Ethan and I will hear him over the loud music of the club.

"Listen here, you pompous, self-entitled rich kid. Fallyn is completely out of your league and wants absolutely nothing to do with you. So, take my advice and stay the fuck away from her. Or else."

"Or else what?" he challenges Emilio. "What're you going to do? I'm the Mayor, remember? I can destroy your life with a single phone call."

"Don't fucking test me, rich boy. Get the hell out of my uncle's bar."

"Is there a problem here?" Alex asks, looking between them.

"Nope, no problem here, Zio. The Mayor was just leaving."

Thinking better of it, Ethan keeps his mouth shut and with a smile, turns on his heel and leaves.

I take a deep breath and turn to go back to serving up drinks when Alex puts his hand on my shoulder.

"You two, we're going to talk later, but for now get your asses to work."

I nod my head and get back to serving drinks to customers.

"Goodnight," I call out to the couple leaving as we lock the doors.

I go back behind the bar to finish washing glasses and wipe everything down while Emilio wipes down tables and flips up chairs.

Tonight was stressful as hell and I have a feeling it's only going to get worse. Alex comes out of the back and looks around to make sure everyone has cleared out.

"You two, over here. Now," he says, pointing at both of us.

Both of us stop what we're doing and walk over to where he's standing.

"You two know this is just going to end in disaster right?" he says, looking between us.

"I… I don't know what you're talking about." I try to play stupid, but he isn't buying it.

Alex starts to butt-in but Emilio cuts him off, "Look, Zio, I realize shit can get really tricky with our relationship but I love her. I've never felt this strongly for a woman before and I'm not about to just give up because Dad or the Chief won't approve. Can we please just keep this between us?"

Alex throws his hands up, "Abso-fucking-lutely. I don't even want your father to know that I know anything about this. When he finds out you're fucking the chief's daughter, he's going to have your head on a platter."

"He'll never know," Emilio promises his uncle.

"Good. Because I rather like my tongue attached and in my mouth, which he will undoubtedly cut out if he finds out I've been lying or withholding information from him. I let them use the bar for their meetings but I stay out of all their 'business dealings', and I'd like to keep it that way."

"He will never know," Emilio assures him.

Alex nods and returns to his office as we finish closing up. After counting cash, I lock it in the safe and say goodnight to Alex before leaving work. Emilio follows me out, unsure if Ethan will be waiting outside.

"You know, I was handling Ethan just fine. You didn't need to get involved."

Spinning me around, he pins me to my car with an arm on either side of my head.

"Yeah, it sure looked like you were handling him," he says cockily. "I told you I'd kill him if he touched you." His eyes darken as the words leave his mouth.

I stand on my toes, wrapping my arms around his neck, letting my lips brush his. "No need for all that. No matter what he does, I'll always be yours." I crush my lips to his and he wraps his arms tight around me.

My phone dings and I break away from him to pull it from my pocket. Checking the notification, there's a text from my father.

*Hey princess, I know you're upset with me right now, but I wanted to let you know the department called and asked me to fly to DC for some training with the FBI.*

*I'll be back in a couple days and then we can talk.*

*Love you princess.*

"The FBI, huh?" Emilio says.

"I guess so." I shrug, opening the door to my SUV and tossing my phone over onto the passenger's seat. "Do you know what that means?"

"What?"

"That means you're coming home with me," I whisper.

"Mmm… sounds like a plan to me. Shall we go?"

Emilio locks up his car and climbs into the passenger seat of my SUV. Hopping into the driver's seat, I fire up the engine and head towards home. The anticipation of what's to come causes my core to heat and when I glance at Emilio, the same passionate fire is reflected in his eyes.

# Chapter 3

## Fallyn

Being able to wake up next to Emilio is incredible. It makes our relationship feel normal like we don't have to hide from the world. It's three in the morning, and I'm wishing for sleep.

Rolling over, I cuddle up next to him; my head on his chest, letting his heartbeat sing me a lullaby. He shifts slightly and runs his hand up and down my back soothingly. I look up and his brown eyes flutter open sleepily.

"You okay, *Bellissima*?" he asks.

"Yea… I'm sorry, I didn't mean to wake you."

"Don't apologize, it's fine," he says, kissing the top of my head.

I lay my head back down on his chest and trace circles on his stomach with my finger.

"What are you thinking about, *mia Regina*?"

"Just how great it is that we don't have to pretend we aren't together. Even if it's just for a couple of days."

"I know, *Bellissima*. We'll figure it out, yeah?"

"Yeah." I sigh, closing my eyes. We lay there in silence, just holding each other as we drift off to sleep.

My alarm sounds a few hours later, startling me out of deep sleep. I reach out for Emilio but he's gone.

Jumping out of bed, I grab my phone from the nightstand and dial his number as I make my way down the stairs. Just as I'm about to hit call, something in the kitchen catches my attention. I silently say a prayer, hoping my father didn't come home early, forcing Emilio sneak out so we wouldn't be caught. Coming around the corner into the kitchen, I'm relieved—Emilio stands at the stove cooking breakfast.

"*Buongiorno, Bellissima.* How did you sleep?"

"I slept well. You?" I wrap my arm around his waist and reach up to kiss him on his cheek.

"I woke up next to you, it was fantastic," he says, smiling down at me before kissing my hair. "Breakfast will be ready soon, go sit."

"Okay."

On my way to sit at the breakfast bar, I grab a bottle of champagne and orange juice from the fridge to make mimosas. I pour us each a glass as he brings our plates to the bar.

"I could totally get used to this," I say, smiling at him.

He grins. "Good."

I dig into the omelet on my plate, "Oh my god, this is so good."

"Anything for *mia Regina*."

I swoon a little at his Italian nickname for me; it means "my queen", and I absolutely love it.

Finishing up my omelet and mimosa, I rinse our dishes and load them into the dishwasher along with the pans. Walking back over to the breakfast bar, I slide in between him and the bar, straddling his lap.

"Is it too early for dessert?" I ask in my best seductive voice.

"Mmm, *Bellissima*, it's never too early."

Placing his hands on either side of my face, he kisses me deeply, passionately, and it makes me instantly wet. I moan against his lips as I grind against his lap. Grabbing for the hem of my shirt, I strip it off and toss it to the floor, exposing my breasts.

"*Perfezionare.*"

He grabs my breasts, gently massaging them and rolling my nipples between his thumb and index finger. A soft moan escapes my lips as my back arches, pressing my breasts into his hands more. Releasing one, he leans down, taking the nipple into his mouth.

He begins a slow assault on it with his tongue, lightly running his teeth across the sensitive skin. I thrust my hands into his hair, lightly tugging on it. Releasing the first nipple, he moves to the other. Placing my hand under his chin, I lift his face, causing him to release my nipple from his mouth.

I press my lips to his, kissing him deeply, letting him know how badly I need him right now. My hands run down his shoulders, to the top button of his dress shirt. I fumble with them as I work my way down, unfastening each one, exposing his muscular chest and stomach. I push the shirt off and he slips his arms out, letting it fall to the floor.

Our lips never lose contact as he stands. I lock my legs around his waist as he undoes his slacks and lets them fall to the floor. I use my heels to help remove his boxers.

He breaks our kiss, leaving both of us panting. "Stand up, *Bellissima*, and lean over the chair."

I lower my feet to the floor, and he holds me until I'm steady. Turning around, I lean over the chair. Hooking his fingers in the sides of my panties, he slides them down my legs and I kick them to the side.

"Spread your legs," he instructs.

I do as I'm told, standing naked and waiting with anticipation. He gives my ass a slap, causing me to yelp.

"Your ass is so perfect, *mia Regina*."

He's quiet, and then his hand lands flat against my sensitive pussy, causing a delicious sting. The yelp I let out turns to a moan when he cups my pussy, softly massaging it. I push back against his hand, needing more. Giving me what I want, he slips two fingers inside me and I gasp.

"You like that?" he asks, sliding his fingers in and out of me.

"Yes."

"Who's pretty little pussy is this?"

"Yours," I moan. "It's all yours, babe."

"Mmm, yes it is." His voice is deep and gravelly now. The tone nearly makes me come in his hand.

"Emilio," I say through gritted teeth, as he picks up the pace, his fingers hitting that sweet spot deep inside me

"Tell me what you want, *mia Regina*? Anything for my queen."

"I want you. I need you inside me. Make love to me, Emilio."

"Your wish is my command, *Bellissima*."

He slowly removes his fingers and pulls me into a standing position. Leading me over to the couch, he sits and pulls me astride him. Lifting myself up on my knees, I wrap my hand around his length and center him at my opening.

Slowly, I ease myself down as he fills me, both of us sucking in air between our teeth. Emilio grabs me by my hips, holding me in place as he slides out of me and then swiftly rams into me causing an intoxicating sensation. Leaning in, I kiss him and take over control, riding him.

He moans into my mouth, then softly bites down on my bottom lip. Working his way across my jawline, he lightly nips at the skin and makes his way down my neck. My body builds, so I pick up the pace. Emilio grabs my ass, digging his fingers into the flesh as I ride him.

"*Mia Regina*, slow down, I'm going to come."

My pussy clenches around him and my legs start to shake. I don't slow down. If anything, I move faster, my orgasm on the brink of eruption. A deep growl comes from Emilio's throat and I watch him find his release. Seeing his face, and knowing I'm the reason for his pleasure, sends me over the edge, and I erupt around him. My orgasm wracks my body and I collapse against his chest with him still inside me. Emilio wraps his arms around me, holding me against his chest and kisses my hair.

"*Ti amo, mia Regina*," he whispers against my hair.

"I love you too, babe."

# Chapter 4

## Fallyn

After the amazing post breakfast sex yesterday, we spent the rest of the day doing pretty much the same. Eat, watch a movie, have sex; there are absolutely no complaints here.

He got a call early this morning that had him calling a cab and leaving. He said he'd stop by the bar later tonight, and I'm just hoping there isn't another incident with Ethan.

Not being able to fall back to sleep, I shower and get ready for my day. Standing at the bay window, I sip my coffee and think about how wonderful the last couple days have been.

My dad's car pulls into the circular driveway and I make my way to the door to greet him. When I swing the door open, I stumble a couple steps back when the man climbing out of the back seat of the car isn't my father.

"What are you doing here, and why are you in my father's car? Where is he?"

"He's having lunch with my father. He suggested I take the car to come and spend some time with you."

"My father was obviously mistaken. Goodbye, Ethan." I go to slam the door in his face but he blocks it with his foot and pushes his way in.

"What are you doing? Get out!" I try to push him back out the door but he's stronger than I am.

Pushing me back, I almost fall on my ass as he shuts the door behind him and locks it.

Turning around, I run to the table and grab my phone. Just as I'm about to dial Emilio, Ethan grabs the phone from my hand and throws it against the wall. It shatters into pieces and falls to the floor.

He pushes me up against the wall, pinning my wrists above my head. He leans in to try to kiss me but I spit in his face. Rage flashes in his eyes, and then he slaps me across my face, hard. My cheek throbs in pain but I refuse to back down and give into him.

"Now, you're going to give me what I want. I won't take no for an answer." With his free hand, he runs it down my body and over my abdomen, grabbing my pussy through my shorts. "I want this."

"You will never get it."

"You sure about that?" he says as he undoes the button on my shorts and slides his hand into my panties.

My head starts to spin as he slides his fingers inside me. I want to cry, scream, I want to fight back against him but he's stronger and bigger than I am. With no other option, as much as it nauseates me, I play along to lure him closer to me.

"Fine, you win," I say, bile rising in my throat with the words.

"I knew you'd see it my way," he says cockily. Releasing my hands, he starts to undo his pants, letting them drop to the floor.

I crook my finger, moving it in a 'come here' motion. He grins and moves closer, wrapping his arms around me. He stands against me, bowlegged, and gives me my opportunity.

I quickly bring my knee up, connecting hard with his genitals. He falls to the floor in agonizing pain. I grab his phone from his pants from the floor and dial my father.

"Mayor, how's it going?"

"Dad, it's me."

"Fallyn, where is Ethan?"

"On the floor holding his fucking nuts. Your perfect-for-me Mayor just tried to rape me. I want to press charges, have some of your guys come hook him up."

"But Fallyn…"

I cut him off. "I don't give a fuck if he's the Mayor, I want him arrested now!"

Hitting end on the phone, I throw it at him. Running to my room, I quickly change before running towards the front door. Unlocking it, I grab my keys from the table next to me. As I make my way out the door, two officers arrive.

"He's inside. I have to go to work, lock up after you leave. You can come to Manzini's to get my statement."

Climbing into my SUV, I buckle in and take off towards Manzini's. I pull into the empty lot, putting my truck in park. I sit there, trying to catch my breath and that's when everything hits me.

I wrap my arms around my stomach as tears stream down my face. What happened plays in my mind and makes me want to vomit.

There's a knock on my window and when I look up into the sexy smile on Emilio's face, it fades quickly and a look of sheer terror replaces it. He quickly opens the door and pulls me out into his arms. He doesn't ask any questions, he just holds me against him as I sob. After the tears start to subside, he slowly releases me.

"What happened, *Bellissima*? Is everything okay?"

I'm silent for a moment, unsure if I should even tell him.

"Talk to me, *Bellissima*. Please," he says as he softly caresses my cheek.

Tears build in my eyes again, "After you left this morning…" I choke down the sob and continue. "My dad's car pulled in, only it wasn't him."

"Who was it, Fallyn?" he says sternly. He never uses my name and it catches me off guard. The anger building in his eyes, tells me he has a pretty clear idea of who it is.

"Ethan."

Emilio stands, silently staring at me but I can tell he's pissed. "What happened?" he asks, his voice is deep, but not in the sexy way like yesterday.

"He-he tried to rape me."

"He what?" Emilio's voice booms, echoing through the neighborhood. "Where is he?" His hands are balled into fists and the vein in his neck is pulsating.

"I called my father; his guys took him into custody."

"Ha." He snarls, "He'll be out by morning."

"I know," I say, my head dropping between my shoulders.

Emilio's footsteps stop and then I'm pulled into his strong arms. "I'm so sorry, *mia Regina*. I should've protected you."

His words cut deep into my heart. "This isn't your fault, Emilio. "

"Yes, it is. It's my job to protect you and I failed. But that ends now. Go inside and lock the door behind you. Get everything set up for opening, I'll call my uncle to make sure you're not alone for too long. I'll be back in a little bit. I love you."

"I love you," I say, standing on my toes to kiss him. "Please don't do anything stupid," I whisper to him.

He just shakes his head, the set of his jaw making me realize nothing I say will stop him now.

Emilio waits until I'm safely inside before he takes off. I breathe a sigh of relief. Even though this is a public nightclub, this is one of the only places I feel safe.

# Chapter 5

## Emilio

Sliding in the front seat of my Camaro, I slam into drive and peel out of the parking lot of Manzini's. Rage pulsating through my veins, I head towards the one place I never thought I'd be going.

I refused to live under my father's thumb and go into the 'family business'—so he gave me an ultimatum; leave and never look back or stay and take over when he steps down. I left and never looked back, until now.

Pulling up in front of the stone mansion, I park in the driveway and make my way inside. When I reach the door, I take a deep breath before turning the knob. I can't believe I'm doing this right now.

Pushing the door open, I step inside the family home where my father does all his business, well, here and Manzini's. Reaching the door to his office, I knock before entering. He's on the phone but waves me in to take a seat.

"Well, I'd be lying if I said I wasn't surprised to see you here," he says as he hangs up the phone. "What can I do for you, son? Did you come back to take over the family business?"

"Not in this lifetime. Or the next."

He chuckles, leaning forward in his chair. "Well then, what do I owe the pleasure of this visit?"

"I want all business with the Mayor shut down immediately!"

My father raises his eyebrow at me, "Why would I do that?"

"He's a liability."

"How so?" he inquires.

"Does it really fucking matter?" my voice booms through the office, frustrated at my father's questioning. "He's a liability, get rid of him."

He chuckles. "Is this about the Chief's daughter you've been fucking?"

"Leave her out of this," I growl.

"I'll make you a deal, son. You break it off with the Chief's little princess and I'll take care of the mayor."

"Absolutely not." I slam my fist on his desk causing his goons to step forward. "I love her. You're out of your mind if you think I'd leave her."

My father pulls a cigar from the box in his drawer. Lighting the end, he takes a long pull and blows out the smoke. "Well, that's your only option. Break things off with the girl, otherwise you can take your ass out of here and not come back."

"You know what… fuck you." Standing, I turn on my heel and storm out. I should've known better than to come here to ask for help. I'll just handle that asshole, Ethan-fucking-Franklyn, myself.

# Chapter 6

## Fallyn

Concentrating on work tonight has proven difficult. How can I concentrate on my work when I don't know where Emilio is and if he's okay? Thankfully, tonight is pretty slow and there's only a couple regulars hanging around.

I'm zoning out behind the bar when his smooth voice comes from the far end. Relief floods through me when I see that he's okay. I tell the customers I'll be right back and excuse myself.

Walking towards Emilio, I slink past him and into Alex's office. I quickly wave him inside and shut the door behind him.

As I spin around to face him, he pins me against the door and his lips are just inches from mine. Framing his face with my hands, I kiss him deeply as our tongues do the tango.

"I was so worried about you," I whisper breathlessly.

"I'm here, *Bellissima.* I'm okay," he says, kissing me again.

Emilio lifts me and I wrap my legs around his hips as he presses his growing erection against my sensitive pussy. I let out a small moan as he wraps his hand up in my hair, pulling my head back to give him access to my neck.

His lips on my skin set me on fire, and I completely forget about the customers until someone knocks on the door to the office.

"Shit," I say through gritted teeth as I release my legs from his waist.

I straighten my clothes and fix my hair before heading back out behind the bar. I grab another round for the customers and apologize for the wait. They don't seem to mind.

Emilio takes a seat at the end of the bar, and I wink at him. A smirk spreads across his beautiful face as his eyes darken. There's an unspoken promise exchanged between us and it instantly makes my already aching pussy a little wetter.

In an effort to distract myself, I grab a rag and start wiping everything down for closing. Slowly, one after the other, customers trickle out the door until they're all gone. I finish wiping down everything while Emilio helps by flipping the chairs up on the bar. I grab my keys out of the office and turn out the lights. Locking up, we make our way to my SUV.

Emilio reaches out, softly caressing my cheek. "How are you, *mia Regina*?"

"I'm okay," I say.

His brows crease. "Are you sure?"

"Yes, I'm sure." I stand on my toes to kiss his lips. "I love you."

"I love you too, *Bellissima.* Let's go back to my place so I can show you how much," he says, brushing my hair back behind my ear.

"Okay."

Locking up my SUV, I climb into the passenger side of his Camaro. He jumps into the driver's seat and we take off towards his place.

On the way, Emilio reaches over, lightly running his hand up and down my thigh; his touch sends a tingling sensation through my body that causes me to squirm. He chuckles and removes his hand as we pull up outside of his house.

Not waiting for him to come around and open my door, I jump out of the car and into his arms when he comes towards me. He kisses me as he walks us towards the door, fumbling to find his key.

Once we're inside, he places me on my feet. I walk over to the stereo, bending over to put on music when he comes up behind me. Grabbing me by my hips, he grinds his erection into my ass and I press back against him.

A growl comes from deep in his throat as he grabs me and pulls me into a standing position, quickly stripping me of my bra and tank top. I help by undoing my cut off shorts before he strips them, along with my panties, down my legs. He takes my hand in his and leads me over to the chair.

"Bend over," he demands, and his no-nonsense tone makes me I do as I'm told.

He's quiet for a minute and I don't know he's on his knees until his mouth is on my aching pussy. His tongue dips inside me, giving my clit a few flicks. I moan his name and feel him grin between my legs before he grazes my clit with his teeth.

The sensation sends a jolt through me and I nearly come just from the masterful use of his mouth. He stands and the room is filled with the jingle of his belt being undone, then the zipper, and his jeans hitting the floor.

Emilio centers himself at my opening and I press back against him, eager to feel him inside me. He doesn't waste any time as he slams into me. Emilio wraps one hand tight in my hair as he holds my waist with the other.

Slowly, he pulls out and slams into me again, eventually settling into a delicious rhythm. Gradually, he picks up speed and his hand on my hip moves to press against my abdomen while pulling on my hair causing my back to arch. His warm breath heats my neck as he whispers things to me in Italian. I don't understand anything he's saying but it all sounds really sexy.

He picks up speed, slamming into me as he nips at my neck. A sound of pure, carnal need escapes my throat as my body builds. His breathing in my ear becomes labored and I know he's close too. My moaning becomes louder as my legs start to shake.

"Faster, Emilio. I'm going to come."

Releasing my hair, he grabs my hips with both hands, digging his fingers into my flesh as he plows into me. A few more thrusts and he grunts behind me as he reaches his orgasm. The sounds of his pleasure, sends me over the edge and I come too.

Emilio carefully pulls out of me, and I immediately feel the loss of having him inside me. Wrapping his arms around me, he pulls me back and holds me against his chest.

"You know I love you, right *Bellissima*?"

I turn my head so I can see him. "I know. I love you too."

"And you know I'd do anything to protect you?"

"Of course." I spin in his arms, and rest my hands on his shoulders. "Where's all this coming from? Because of what happened with Ethan? That wasn't your fault," I remind him.

He casts his eyes to the floor, attempting to avoid eye contact with me.

"Babe, it's okay. I'm fine," I try to reassure him.

He lets out a frustrated breath before turning away from me to grab his jeans and pull them on. Suddenly feeling self-conscious, I grab my clothes off the floor and get dressed. Emilio begins to pace back and forth, his bare feet padding against the floor.

"I'm sorry," I apologize, because I don't know what else to do. "You shouldn't be in the middle of this. I know Ethan does business with your father."

Emilio stops dead in his tracks, staring at me, his brows creased in confusion. "You think I'm upset that our relationship could cause issues for my father and his 'business'?"

The frustration and anger in his voice catches me off guard and all I can do is shrug. I cast my eyes to the floor as he approaches me. Lifting my chin with his finger, he forces me to look at him.

"I'm not upset with you, *mia Regina*. My frustration has nothing to do with Ethan doing business with my father." He pauses before continuing, "I'm frustrated with myself."

Now I'm the one confused. "What? Why?"

"When I walked up to your SUV and found you sobbing, it tore my heart out. Then you told me what Ethan did and I wanted to kill him. All I felt was pure fucking rage and I wanted him dead. I wanted to go to him and blow his fucking brains out, not thinking twice about it. In that moment, I realized I'm just like him…"

"You are nothing like Ethan…"

"Not Ethan. My *father*."

"You're wrong. You are *nothing* like your father. He murders people when he doesn't get his way, you were angry about what happened to *me*. It's a natural reaction and you didn't kill Ethan."

"I would have, had he not been in police custody."

"That still doesn't make you like your father."

Walking over to him, I wrap my arms around his waist and rest my head on his chest. Emilio runs his hand through my long brunette hair, before kissing me on the head and tightening his arms around me.

"If anything else ever happens to you, I'm not sure anyone could stop me from hurting someone," he whispers against my hair.

# Chapter 7

## Fallyn

I sit on the couch, sipping a cup of coffee and thinking about last night. My heart aches for Emilio and his internal battle with not wanting to become a monster like his father. The thing is, he's nothing like his father. I just wish he could see himself the way I do.

A noise comes from the doorway of the bedroom catching my attention. Glancing up, I find Emilio leaning against the door frame watching me. He's shirtless and wearing a pair of sweatpants that show off his impressive bulge.

I lick my lips as my eyes move from his pants back up to his face. A smirk spreads across his face and he intentionally adjusts himself. Cheeky fucker.

"What were you so deep in thought about?" he asks as he makes his way over to sit with me.

"Nothing really."

"Are you sure, *Bellissima*? You know you can tell me anything."

"I'm sure." I smile up at him. "So, how did you— hey, that's mine, get your own," I say, as he steals my coffee out of my hands.

"Mmm… but yours is so much better."

I roll my eyes at him. "You're lucky I love you."

"I know." Leaning in, he places a quick kiss to my lips before handing me back my coffee and going to fix his own.

A few moments later, he's back on the couch next to me. "So, what do you want to do today? You're off, right?"

I shrug. "Yea, I'm off. We can do whatever you want."

That devious smile is back, as he slides his hand up my thigh. "Well, I do have something in mind, but it doesn't involve leaving the house."

"We aren't staying in all day. I want to go out. I'm tired of hiding our relationship."

"Me too, *Bellissima*. We'll go out… after breakfast."

He moves from the couch to kneel in front of me. Looping his fingers into the sides of my panties, he quickly slides them down my legs. Crumpling them up in his hand, he brings them up to his nose, breathing in my scent.

"You smell so sweet, *Bellissima*," he says as he tosses them to the floor. "Spread your legs."

Lying against the back of the couch, I spread my legs.

"Such a pretty little pussy," he says, running the tip of his finger along my slit. Bringing the finger to his mouth, he sucks my wetness from it. "Mmm, you taste so sweet."

His voice is deep, seductive, and just listening to him makes me want to combust. Sliding his arms under my thighs, he lifts my legs over his shoulders. He leans in and his tongue darts between his lips, giving my clit a quick flick that makes my body buck and causes me to whimper.

He brings his hand up, spreading my pussy lips as he dips his tongue inside me. Moaning, I thrust my hands into his hair to hold him in place as his tongue continues its delicious torture of circular motions.

Removing his mouth, he slips two fingers inside me, pumping them in and out of me in rapid succession. My back arches with every thrust of his fingers as my body builds and I moan loudly.

"Who's pretty little pussy is this, *mia Regina*?"

"Yours… Oh god, it's all yours. Please don't stop."

"Never. I love watching you come undone for me."

My pussy clenches around his fingers as he picks up speed.

"Come for me, *Bellissima*."

A few more pumps of his fingers and I'm falling over the edge. Emilio quickly removes his fingers from me, replacing his mouth where they just were. I thrust my hands into his hair again, pulling it lightly as I hold him in place with my thighs. He doesn't stop or try to pull away. He continues to fuck me with his tongue, drinking in my orgasm until my body stills and my legs stop shaking.

I collapse back into the couch, closing my eyes and breathing heavily. I can feel Emilio staring at me and I slowly open my eyes to find him sitting on his heels, still kneeling in front of me.

"So, did you enjoy your breakfast? Because I sure enjoyed mine."

He chuckles. "Most definitely, *Bellissima.* I enjoyed every little bit of it." Emilio gets to his feet and reaches out his hand to me, "Come on, let's go shower and then go to a movie and dinner."

"Okay." I take his hand, letting him lead me into the bathroom so we can get ready for our first time out as a couple.

Showered and ready, we lock up the house and climb into Emilio's Camaro. Pulling out of the driveway, we take off towards the local theater to see what's playing. I turn the radio up and stare out the window, watching the trees and buildings pass by when I notice a car that's been following us since we left Emilio's house. I turn in my seat to look out the back window, trying to get a better look at who might be driving.

"Everything okay?"

"That car behind us. It's been following us since we left your place."

Emilio stares into the rearview mirror and clenches his jaw. "Are you sure?"

"Yes, I'm sure."

"Okay." Emilio pulls onto a side street and the black Lincoln follows. Pulling into a parallel spot, Emilio puts the car in park and undoes his seatbelt.

"What are you doing?"

"I'm going to confront them." He reaches for the door but I grab his hand.

"Please don't, let's just call my father and let him handle it."

"Stay here."

Without another word, Emilio climbs out of the car to confront whoever has been following us. I watch in horror as the front driver's side door opens on the Lincoln and Ethan Franklyn steps out of the car, and they exchange words.

Ethan looks at me, blowing me a kiss and my stomach churns. There's another exchanging of words then within a second, Emilio picks Ethan up, slamming him up against the side of his car. Scrambling to undo my seatbelt, I jump out of the car.

"Emilio! Please stop!" I scream as he pulls his fist back and swings, connecting with Ethan's face knocking him to the ground.

"Fallyn, get back in the car," he growls at me.

I ignore him, as tears begin to stream down my face. Ethan tries to stand up but Emilio kicks him in the gut, causing him to hit the ground again.

Emilio kneels over him, pulling him up by his shirt and punches him again as blood spurts from Ethan's nose. "I told you to stay away from her, but you just couldn't heed my warning. She's mine and if you touch her again, I'll kill you."

A bloody smirk spreads across Ethan's face. "That little pussy has you hooked, huh? I don't blame you, she sure does taste sweet. I can still taste that sweet little pussy on my fingers. Go ahead and have your fun, but she will be mine."

Emilio quickly reaches under his pant leg and I gasp when he pulls a gun from an ankle holster and aims it at the Mayor.

"You willing to bet your life on it?"

Fear spreads across Ethan's face as he furiously shakes his head no. "I'm sorry, I'm sorry. I'll stay away, I promise."

I rush to Emilio's side, grabbing a hold of his arm. "Babe, please," I beg him. "He isn't worth it, just let it go. This isn't who you are."

He looks at Ethan and then back at me, his face softening a touch. Placing a kiss to my temple, he turns his attention back to Ethan.

"This is your last warning. If you even so much as glance in her direction, I promise you, it'll be the last thing you ever see. Do you understand?"

"Yes, I-I understand," Ethan stutters through his words as he scrambles to his feet. He quickly climbs into his car and peels off down the street. We both watch until his taillights disappear.

# Chapter 8

## Emilio

The adrenaline pumps through my veins like electricity through water as his taillights disappear around the corner. I take a deep breath and turn to look at Fallyn. My heart breaks as I take in the look on her face, a look of pure fear. Seeing her scared like that, tears me apart. I've become the monster I swore I'd never be.

My head sinks between my shoulders. "I'm sorry," I mutter because I don't know what else to say.

She doesn't say anything, but her soft hand caresses my face. "Let's get out of here," she whispers.

I nod my head as we walk towards the car and climb inside. Opening the center console, I place the gun inside and shut it. My altercation ruining the mood for our date, I fire up the engine of my Camaro and head back towards my place.

Pulling into the driveway, we make our way inside and I grab a bottle of wine from the fridge. I pour us both a glass and take a seat on the couch next to Fallyn, handing her a glass.

We sit in silence, just staring at the blank screen of the television before she breaks the silence.

"You're still nothing like him," she says, as if she's reading my mind.

I let my head fall back against the couch. "Yes, I am. I was one snarky ass comment from pulling the trigger. I'm a monster, just like him."

Her glass clinks on the coffee table before she climbs into my lap and forces me to look at her. When I do, her eyes are full of tears threatening to stream down her pretty face.

"You're no monster, Emilio. There is a difference between protecting someone you love and being a cold blooded killer. Besides, if you were really a monster like your father, I wouldn't have been able to stop you from pulling the trigger."

"How do you know? That lifestyle is all I knew growing up. Trafficking drugs and illegal weapons. Killing people when they didn't do exactly as they were told, as they begged and pleaded for their lives."

"Want to know how I know? I know because you chose to walk away from that life, and you've been surviving on your own without any help from them. You're sweet, kind, and compassionate. Your father, he's none of that."

"I love you, *mia Regina*," I say, placing a kiss on her forehead.

"I love you," she says, pressing her soft, sweet lips to mine.

I lightly bite her lip and she gasps as I slip my tongue into her mouth. Our tongues do a dance as I wrap my hands up in her hair, holding her to me. She rocks against my lap, letting me know she wants it too. I reach for the hem of her shirt just as there's a knock at the door.

"Fuck," I growl, moving her off my lap onto the couch. Standing, I adjust myself before answering the door.

When I swing the door open, I'm met by officers with guns in my face.

"Son of a bitch," I mutter under my breath.

Fallyn springs from the couch and is standing at my side.

"What the hell is this about?"

"I'm sorry, Fallyn. We have to take him in. The Mayor is accusing Emilio of attacking him and pulling a gun on him."

"Are you fucking kidding me?" she shouts at the officers and the one cringes causing me to chuckle.

"*Bellissima*, it's okay. Just meet us at the station. I love you."

"I love you. I'll be there," she says, standing on her toes to kiss me before they cuff me and walk me to the cruiser.

# Chapter 9

## Fallyn

I grab Emilio's keys from the table and dial my father on the way to the car. Sliding into the driver's seat, I peel out of the driveway and haul ass towards the jail.

The line rings three times before voicemail picks up; dammit. Frustrated, I toss my phone into the passenger's seat. The ten minute drive to the station feels like forever. Pulling into the lot, I put the car in park and sprint inside.

"Hello, Fallyn," the receptionist says cheerfully.

"Hi, Camille. I need to see my father. Now."

She nods her head and dials his extension. "Hey, Chief. Your daughter is here to see you." She pauses for a moment before saying okay and hanging up the receiver.

"He'll be out in just a moment if you want to take a seat."

"Okay, thank you."

Not being able to sit, I pace the lobby until the door to my right opens.

"Fallyn." My father waves me into the back.

We walk in silence to his office and I close the door behind us as we enter.

"You need to drop the charges against Emilio Manzini."

"Oh yea, why is that?" he asks, his voice calm and steady.

"He was protecting me! He didn't do anything wrong."

"But he had a gun…" his voice trails off.

"Yes, legally!" I pull his wallet from my pocket and flip it open to his concealed weapons permit.

My father clenches his jaw and I know the questions are coming.

"What're were doing with him, Fallyn, and why do you have his wallet?"

"That's none of your damn business. Last time I checked, I'm twenty-five and don't have to disclose everything I do, or who I'm spending time with, to you."

"You do when you're spending time with the son of a man I'm trying to take down. So, I'm going to ask you again… What were you doing with him?"

"Fucking him. I was fucking the shit out of him because he's my boyfriend."

His face turns beat red and it looks like his head might explode. "I forbid you to see him, he's just like his father."

"You know nothing about him! He is nothing like his father, one thing we have in common," I say snarkily.

That jab hits him where it hurts and he softens slightly.

"I just want what's best for you, Fallyn. You don't need to be getting mixed up with the likes of him. His family is dangerous."

"The Mayor is dangerous, Dad. Emilio is kind and sweet, and he loves me! If you would just get to know him."

"Honey, when you come from a family like that, it's ingrained in their blood."

"That's not true." I try to choke back the sobs that threaten. Hearing him talk about Emilio this way is killing me.

"He's a good man, Dad. He wants nothing to do with his family, especially his father."

He doesn't say anything, he just stares at me with a conflicted expression.

"Wasn't it you that told me, it isn't where you come from, it's where you're going? Just because he comes from a bad family, doesn't mean anything when he wants to do better, be better."

"His family isn't just a bad family. They're a dangerous family. They're mob affiliated. People don't just walk away from them without severe repercussions. What if his father decides he isn't giving Emilio a choice anymore? Then what?"

"He won't and even if he did, Emilio isn't willing to live that kind of life. He's a good person, Daddy. He would never put me in harm's way or let anything happen to me."

That conflicted look is in his eyes again. "Ethan will protect you, too. He assured me he would always keep you safe."

I scoff. "Yea, he'd keep me safe alright, but who's going to keep me safe from him?"

"What's that supposed to mean?"

"Do you seriously not remember yesterday? Has it already slipped your mind that he tried to rape me when you let him use your car to come see me? Have you forgotten that I want to press charges against him for what he did to me?"

Tears swell in his eyes as the words resonate in his mind. "I'm so sorry, princess. Of course I didn't forget, but Ethan swears it was all just a misunderstanding."

"Misunderstanding my ass. That asshole tried to rape me, and now he's out to screw over Emilio. You may think he's a great guy but there is no way in hell I would marry Ethan Franklyn."

My father closes his eyes and runs his hands over his face.

"You need to drop the charges against Emilio. Ethan was following us and when Emilio pulled over to confront him, Ethan antagonized him. Emilio was just defending himself, and me, for what Ethan did to me yesterday."

"Okay. I'll see what I can do. But can you please, just go home and stay there for now? I will keep you updated on what's going on."

"Okay, thank you. I love you," I say, throwing my arms around his neck, giving him a big hug.

Leaving his office, I wave goodbye to Camille as I head out the door. Sliding into the driver's seat of Emilio's Camaro, I head towards home to wait for my father's call.

# Chapter 10

## Emilio

The officers lead me into the intake area and place me in a cell. I sit on the bench, my head in my hands, wishing I wouldn't have been so stupid. What the fuck was I thinking, pulling a gun on him?

"Well, well, well, look what we have here…" the cocky tone ignites the rage within me again and I look up to find the Mayor with a smug grin on his face.

I laugh and shake my head in disbelief, this son of a bitch doesn't quit.

Standing, I stride over to where he's standing. "Get the fuck out of here."

"Oh, don't worry. I am. I just had to make sure the animal was caged before I go retrieve my girl."

"Stay the fuck away from her."

He laughs. Leaning in, he keeps his voice low so only I can hear him. "You've fucked with the wrong person. I always get what I want, willing or forcefully. You'll be here, stuck in a cage, while I tear that pretty little pussy up. I really hope she puts up a fight, I like it when they're feisty."

"You sick son of a bitch!" I snatch his shirt through the bars, slamming him against them.

The guards run to his aid.

"It's okay. I'm okay." he assures the guard.

After the guard walks away, he leans in again but still far enough away that I can't grab him again.

"That's okay. Once I'm finished with her, I'll pass her to my buddies. Maybe even on to your father and his goons, I'm sure they'd love to have a little taste of her."

Bile rises in my throat and anger pulses through my veins but I do my best not to let him get the best of me again.

"Enjoy your cage, Emilio," he says as he turns and walks out of the building.

I slam my fists against the bars, frustrated and feeling helpless. I've got to get out of here.

# Chapter 11

### Fallyn

Pulling into the driveway of the house, I grab my bag off the floor in front of the passenger seat and make my way inside. I grab the remote off the table and flip on the television to a music channel while I pour myself glass a wine.

Sitting on the couch, I begin channel surfing, trying to distract myself. An hour into a marathon of some lame reality show, my phone rings. Checking the caller ID, I see it's my father.

"Hey, daddy," I answer.

"Hey, princess. The charges have been dropped against Emilio and he's being released. He might still face some blowback for assaulting the mayor though."

"I understand."

"Good. He'll be out soon, I'll tell him where you are."

"Thanks, Daddy."

"Anything for my princess."

Hanging up the phone, I jump up and down in excitement.

"Mmm… I was hoping you'd be excited to see me." Ethan's voice stops me dead in my tracks and my stomach flip flops.

"How did you get in here?" I ask him, backing away.

"I have my ways," he says, slithering towards me.

I turn to run, but he grabs my arm snatching me back against him.

"Look, you little bitch, you're going to stop running from me."

"Stop. Let me go!" I scream at him, struggling to get away. I dig my nails into his flesh and he lets go, giving me a chance to run. I run for the door, trying to get outside to yell for help but when I reach out for the knob, Ethan jumps in front of me.

"Just where do you think you're going? We're going to have a little fun."

"The fuck we are," I say, spitting in his face. Ethan brings his hand back and slaps me hard across the face, knocking me to the ground.

"I've had enough of this shit," he says, kicking me in my ribs.

The pain is excruciating and I curl into a ball, praying for Emilio to show up. Ethan's pants hit the ground and I try to crawl away before he grabs me and pins me down. Pushing my skirt up, he loops his finger in the crotch of my panties and with one swift movement rips them from my body.

A million different thoughts run through my head, and I try to come up with some way to escape. I look around the room for anything I can grab to hit him with when I spot my purse on the floor, the glistening steel of Emilio's gun glinting inside.

When he put it into the console, it must have fallen into my bag. Ethan reaches for his pants, lifting his weight off me slightly and I take the chance to get away.

Using all the strength in my legs, I manage to flip him off me. Jumping to my feet, I run to my purse and pull the gun from my bag. Ethan grabs my shoulder and I spin around pointing the gun in his face.

"Now who's the bitch," I smirk at him.

He chuckles. "You aren't going to shoot me."

I repeat Emilio's words from earlier, "You willing to bet your life on it?"

# Chapter 12

## Emilio

I lay in my cell staring at the ceiling, contemplating how the fuck I'm going to get out of this cage when the cell door slides open.

"Emilio Manzini, you're free to go."

"Thank you, Chief."

"You're welcome."

"Do you know where Fallyn is?"

"Yes, she's at the house. She's worried sick about you. Come on, I'll give you a ride."

I follow the Chief out to his car and slide into the passenger's seat.

"I have to say, growing up, I never thought I'd be in the front seat of a police car."

Chief Monroe chuckles. "Honestly, neither did I."

We pull out of the parking lot and head towards my girl's house. An awkward silence spreads between us on the ride and I feel the need to assure him that Fallyn is in good hands.

"Chief?"

"Yes?"

"I just need you to know that I understand I'm not the first person you'd choose for your daughter to be with. Hell, I'm not even sure I'd choose me if I was in your shoes. But, I am madly in love with your daughter. When I first pursued her, I knew our relationship would be complicated, for the lack of a better word, but she is worth every ounce of bullshit we have to go through to be together. I love her more than my own life, and I would risk everything to keep her safe and out of harm's way."

"I know, and I can't say that I'm happy about this relationship you two have going on but she loves you, probably as much as you love her. She sees the good in you, and Fallyn has always been a good judge of character. So, I'm going to trust her judgment when it comes to you as well. Just don't make me regret it."

I hold up my right hand. "Scouts honor," I say causing us both to laugh.

The car slows and we turn into the driveway of their house and I immediately spot a shiny black Mercedes parked out front.

"Fuck!"

Before the chief can stop the car, I open the door and spring from the seat, racing for the front door. All I see is fire and there is no doubt in my mind, this time, I'll kill him.

# Chapter 13

## Fallyn

Ethan's jaw tightens and a moment later, he lunges at me, trying to fight the gun out of my hand. Just then, Emilio and my father burst through the door of the house.

"Fallyn!" Emilio rushes towards me as the gun goes off, causing both Emilio and Ethan to hit the ground.

My hand comes up to cut off the scream coming out of my mouth. As the gun hits the floor, my father wraps me up in his arms.

"I'm so sorry, princess. Are you okay?" he says, releasing me to look me over.

I ignore him and rush over to Emilio's side. "Emilio, oh my God," I sob, holding my chest.

Suddenly, Ethan's lifeless body is flipped onto the floor and Emilio slowly gets to his feet, pulling me up with him. Placing my hands on his shoulders, I look him over and find that the only blood on him is Ethan's. Relief rushes over me and I succumb to my tears. Emilio scoops me up in his arms and carries me to the couch.

"Shhh, *Bellissima.* I'm okay, you're okay."

"I-I thought I… I killed you," I choke out between sobs.

"No, *mia Regina*, I'm fine."

My father's voice catches my attention and when I look up, he's standing behind Emilio with his hand on his shoulder.

"Thank you," he says to Emilio, reaching out to shake his hand.

Emilio takes his hand, shaking it. "You're welcome."

"Get her out of here, I'll take care of all this."

"Thank you," Emilio says, shaking my father's hand again.

"Take care of our girl."

"No worries, she's in good hands."

I give my father a tight hug before Emilio leads me out the door. I turn around, mouthing *I love you* to my father, and he blows me a kiss, waving goodbye. We climb into Emilio's car and take off towards his place.

Finally, everything is just the way it should be.

# Chapter 14

## Fallyn

I cuddle into Emilio's side, laying my head on his shoulder. The past few weeks with him have been amazing. No more sneaking around. Not having to hide our relationship from my father anymore feels like a weight has been lifted off my shoulders. I hated lying to him, but Emilio is a good man and I wasn't going to let my father's hatred for his family ruin what we have.

"What're you thinking about, *Bellisima*?"

"How much I love not having to lie to my father about us anymore."

"Me too," he says, kissing my forehead. "I have some errands I have to run today, will you be okay here by yourself for a little bit?"

"Mhm," I answer sleepily. Emilio slides out from underneath me and places a sweet kiss to my lips before he gets ready and leaves.

I pull his pillow against my chest, breathing in the scent of his cologne. I try to go back to sleep but there's no use; I can't sleep without him next to me.

Climbing out of bed, I slip on a pair of his boxers and one of his t-shirts, and make my way to the kitchen to find something to eat. I find some eggs and bacon in the fridge and cook some up for myself.

Grabbing a bottle of water from the fridge and my plate from the counter, I take a seat at the table and dig into my food. As I'm finishing up, the front door opens.

"Babe, do you want some breakfast?" I call out but no one answers.

There is a sudden sickness in the pit of my stomach as I quietly grab Emilio's gun out of the drawer in the kitchen. I walk softly towards the foyer, gun raised, and find the front door open but no one around.

Taking a deep breath, I lower the gun as I shut the door. Suddenly, there's a noise on the stairs and look up to find a man dressed in all black, wearing a mask, coming down the stairs.

I quickly raise the gun and fire. The bullet hits him in the arm and he stumbles back against the wall before regaining his footing. He rushes down the stairs just as another man bursts through the door and grabs me, taking the gun and covering my mouth.

"What the hell happened to you?" the man holding me asks the other.

"What the hell does it look like? The bitch shot me!"

"Mmm, a feisty one, huh? I knew Emilio liked the fiery ones."

"Come on, we have to get out of here before he gets back."

The man holding me moves his hand from my mouth, replaces it with a gag, and quickly blindfolds me. I fight to get away but they overpower me and next thing I know, I'm being shoved into some kind of car.

I try to remain calm but panic takes over and I silently weep. Things have been so great the past few weeks, I was foolish to think the mayor was our only problem.

# Chapter 15

## Emilio

I pull up in front of the police station and make my way inside, a ball of nerves in my stomach. Even though everything is okay between me and the chief, I'm sure I'm still his least favorite person to see, but what I've got to talk to him about is important. Walking into the building, I'm greeted by the receptionist.

"Hi. How can I help you?"

"I'm here to see the chief."

"Is he expecting you?"

"Not exactly."

"Okay, take a seat for a moment and I'll call to see if he's available."

Walking over, I take a seat in one of the chairs and wait. A few moments later, the chief appears at the door.

"Come on back, Emilio."

I take a deep breath and wipe my sweaty palms on my jeans before standing and following him into the back to his office. He waves me into the small room, closing the door behind us. I take a seat across from him and try to remember to breathe.

"So, what can I do for you, Emilio?"

"You've expressed your feelings about Fallyn and I being together, I get it. But Chief, I love her more than I could ever put into words. I'd lay down my life if it meant no harm would ever come to her. Fallyn is the epitome of everything that is right and good in the world, and I can't imagine a moment of not having her in my life. So, Chief Monroe, what I came here for is to ask for your blessing for me to ask Fallyn to be my wife."

The chief is quiet for longer than I like as he thinks about what I've just said. The longer he's quiet, the more the anxiety in my stomach grows.

Finally, after a few minutes, he speaks. "Emilio, you're right. I'm not exactly jumping for joy that Fallyn picked you to fall in love with… but… my girl, she's smart, beautiful, understanding. You know when I first found out about the two of you, I freaked out but Fallyn, she wasn't hearing it. She put me right in my place."

He chuckles to himself. "She sees the good in you, she made me see the good in you. You're a good man, Emilio, and I know you'll do whatever it takes to keep her safe. Always. So yes, I'll give you my blessing."

I breathe out a sigh of relief and reach out to shake the chief's hand. "Thank you."

He nods in acknowledgement.

"Well, I better get home. Fallyn is probably wondering where I am. I'm actually surprised she hasn't called yet."

"Okay. Tell my girl I love her and I'd like to have dinner, the three of us, soon."

"You got it."

Just as I reach for the door, there is a frantic knock before it swings open.

"Chief, you need to come see this. Both of you do."

Panic rises in my throat as we both rush out of the office into one of the meeting rooms. The officer that came to get us clicks a few buttons on the computer and a video pops up on the screen.

It's Fallyn.

"Isn't she pretty?" the masked man asks, tucking a piece of hair behind Fallyn's ear. She jumps and moves out of his touch, struggling against her restraints.

Moving behind her, he undoes the gag and removes the blindfold from her eyes. She blinks a few times, her eyes red from crying. Rage boils my blood as we continue to watch the video.

"Daddy, Emilio. I'm okay. I love you both so much and I'm so sorry."

Sorry? She doesn't have anything to be sorry for! These bastards took her, and I have a feeling I know who's behind it all.

"Daddy, please help me," she pleads into the camera. My heart aches for her. I promised the chief I'd keep her safe, and then this happens.

"That's enough," the man growls, gagging and blindfolding her again.

"Now, listen carefully… if you want your little princess back in one piece, I suggest you do exactly as you're told. Chief Monroe, pull all of your officers that are watching the Manzini property. If they aren't gone within the next thirty minutes, I'll shoot them one-by-one, the last being your sweet girl here.

"As for you, Emilio, your father would like to speak with you. Make sure none of your new found friends follow along, otherwise the only way you'll be getting your girl back is a piece at a time."

The video cuts to black as the rage overtakes all my senses. Just who I expected. I turn to face the chief and he shakes his head at me.

"Absolutely not," he says, as if he's reading my thoughts. "Who's to say he won't just kill you both as soon as you walk through that door?"

"If there is the tiniest chance I can save her, I have to go see what he wants."

The chief barks off orders for someone to pull all detail from my father's house, and then turns his attention back to me. "Fine. But first, come with me."

# Chapter 16

## Fallyn

Panic rises in me as I listen to the masked man in the room. Eli Manzini? But why? What does he have to gain from kidnapping me?

Then it hits me. Emilio. He'll do whatever his father wants as long as he doesn't hurt me. I can't let that happen.

"I want to talk to Eli Manzini," I announce, not even sure if anyone else is in the room.

"Eli is preparing to handle some business with his son."

"I don't care what he's doing. I want to see him. Now."

The man chuckles. "Fine. I'll let him know."

I listen as the footsteps descend. I'm not sure what I'm even going to say to him, but I can't let him turn Emilio into a monster like him to save me. Footsteps approach again, stopping right next to me.

I look up in the dim light as my eyes focus on the man before me. He has an authoritative stance, his features dark and brooding, just like Emilio's. He stares at me, not saying a word. He doesn't have to though, I know exactly who he is.

"Such a pretty girl." I jerk away as he runs his hand down my cheek. "I guess I have you to thank for turning my son into a pussy."

"I didn't turn him into anything. Emilio is exactly the man he should be."

"A pussy of a man," he chuckles to himself. "So, what do you want?"

"Whatever it is you want Emilio to do, I'll do it."

He raises a brow at me, "Why would you do that?"

"Because, I won't let you ruin him when he's worked so hard to become everything you're not."

"Why should I trust that you can get the job done?"

"Because, I'm the chief's daughter and there's nothing he won't do to keep me safe."

He taps his chin. "I'm intrigued."

Without warning, he pulls his hand back and slaps me hard across my face, splitting my lip. My face throbs from the pain but I take a deep breath and reign in the tears. I need to do this. Licking the blood from my lip, I square my shoulders and look him dead in the eye.

"I'm impressed," he says as he leans in so his mouth is near my ear. "Just know, if you fail, I'll kill all of you."

"I won't fail."

Reaching down behind me, he undoes the restraints on my wrists.

"Follow me."

# Chapter 17

## Emilio

I slide into my Camaro and gun it towards my father's house, praying I'm not too late. The chief insisted I get suited up with a ballistics vest before I left the station. Just in case. The whole ride all I think of is Fallyn and how I had planned to propose to her this weekend.

Now, I might not get that chance. *No. Stop it, don't think like that. She's going to be fine*, I tell myself. As I pull into the drive, there's a blacked out SUV parked in the front. As I slow to a stop, four of my father's goons lead Fallyn to the SUV.

"No. No, no, no." I slam my car into park and jump out.

"Fallyn!" I shout, running towards them.

Two more of my father's goons seem to come out of nowhere, armed with assault rifles and aim them at me.

"Fallyn! *Bellisima*, I'm here," I call to her but she doesn't respond.

Her face is stoic as she climbs into the backseat of the blacked out SUV. The four guys that were with her climb into the truck too and they take off.

"Fallyn! Fallyn!" I call out as the SUV disappears in the distance.

The two goons blocking me lower their guns.

"Where is he?" I growl, pushing past them and rushing into the house in search of my father. It doesn't take me long to find him, sitting at his desk in his office.

"Tell me where they're taking her!" I demand.

"They aren't taking her anywhere. She's the one in charge, they're there for her protection."

"What?" I ask confused.

"She volunteered to do whatever I tell her to, so long as I promise not to hurt you." He laughs. "Who knew the little pussy that has you whipped would be a better villain than the boss' son."

Realization hits me. She thinks she's saving me from becoming him.

"Fuck!" I shout, pounding my fists on his desk. His security steps forward but he waves them off. "Fine. You win. Bring her back here, right now. I'll break everything off with her and come back to the family."

My father throws his head back in laughter. "Not a chance."

"Why? Isn't that what you wanted, me to come back to the family?"

"It was, but I can't trust you now that you've made friends with the police. But as long as I have Fallyn, I can get you and the chief to do anything I want. Plus, she'll do whatever I tell her to, to keep you from turning into a monster like me."

# Chapter 18

## Fallyn

A tear streams down my cheek and I swipe it away quickly before anyone can notice. All I wanted to do was run to Emilio but I knew if I tried, Eli Manzini would've killed us both.

The sleek black 9mm lies in my lap as I fight back the bile rising in my throat and my heart nearly beats out of my chest. I don't know if I can do this, but if I don't, me and everyone I love are as good as dead.

The SUV slowly rolls to a stop and when I look out the window, we're just out of sight of a small cottage in the middle of nowhere.

One of Eli's goons slides out of the SUV and helps me out.

"You're up. Remember, if you fail, you die… along with Emilio and your father."

I tuck the gun into the back of my jeans and make my way towards the cottage. Two of the goons follow behind at a distance, probably to make sure I don't chicken out.

As I approach the house, all the lights are off. I carefully try the front door to see if it's unlocked but it isn't, so I quietly make my way around the house, looking for any way to get inside. Getting around to the back, I find a sliding door that's unlocked.

I quietly slip inside, leaving it ajar so I can get away quickly if anything happens. I tiptoe through the family room, trying to be quiet as possible when I slam my knee into the coffee table. I bite my lip and suck in a breath to calm the pain. A light in the bedroom flips on and I duck into the far dark corner, out of sight.

The scraping of a drawer opening and then closing comes from the room, and then the light goes out. I pull the gun from my jeans, pointing it towards the doorway as a dark shadow exits the room into the hallway. It's a woman with long dark hair.

I make my way quietly towards the hallway when there's a creek in the floor and the woman spins around to face me, holding a gun in my face. As my eyes focus in on her face, recognition hits me and sucks all the oxygen from my lungs. She slowly lowers the gun as I try to make sense of what I'm seeing.

"Ma… Mom?"

"Fallyn, what are you doing here?" she asks, grabbing my arm and pushing me into a large storage closet.

"I-I don't understand. I thought you were dead."

"I can explain everything… but first, I need to know how you got here."

"Eli Manzini… he-he ordered a hit on you."

"How did you get mixed up with Eli Manzini?"

"His son Emilio is my boyfriend."

"Did you come here alone?"

"No, I was escorted by four of Eli's bodyguards. I-I was ordered to kill you."

"Then that's what you're going to do."

"What? No, I can't."

"You have to. Eli will kill you if you don't."

"Mom, please don't make me do this," I sob.

"It's the only way. I love you, princess, and I'm so sorry about all of this."

Heavy footsteps sound on the hardwood floor and panic rises within me. My mother covers my mouth, hushing me. We wait until the footsteps descend. Releasing me, she pushes me out the door.

"Now, you have to do it now."

"I can't!" I cry.

"Now, Fallyn!"

My hands trembling, I slowly raise the gun and point it at my mother's chest. I can barely see through my tears as my mother whispers, 'Do it, I love you.'

I pull the trigger; one, two, three times. Her body lifelessly falls to the floor as heavy sobs wreck my body. Eli's bodyguards come rushing into the house at the sound of the gun shots.

"It's done. Now take me home."

They look to my mother's still body and nod before leading me out of the cottage and back to the SUV. Sliding into the back seat, I pull my knees to my chest and sob into my hands.

I can't believe I just killed my own mother in cold blood. It's a silent ride back to the mansion. The SUV rolls to a stop and the bodyguards climb out of the truck and open my door. I slide out. Noticing Emilio's SUV still out front, I rush inside. The goons escort me back to the room where they were holding me before.

"Eli will be with you soon," the one guy says before leaving the room.

I sit in the chair as shock takes over my body. A million different questions run through my mind.

Obviously, Eli knew my mother was alive, but did my dad know? Did Emilio know? Would they keep a secret like this from me?

My emotions are all over the place and I don't know what to think. After what feels like forever, someone clears their throat, grabbing my attention.

"Well, seems as though I underestimated you. You're even more cold hearted than I am, killing your own mother and all."

"Fuck you."

"Is that any way to speak to someone who is sparing your life?"

"Where's Emilio?"

"He's waiting outside for you."

"Can I go?"

"Of course, I never break a promise."

# Chapter 19

## Emilio

My heart is racing and I feel like it's going to burst out of my chest while waiting for Fallyn. Finally, she exits the house and I grab her, wrapping her up in my arms. There's no way in hell I will ever let her out of my sight again.

Releasing Fallyn, I take her hand in mine and we rush towards the car. I constantly keep an eye over our shoulder. Knowing my father, even being a mob boss is too much of a bitch to look someone in the eye as he kills them.

We reach my car and I usher Fallyn into the passenger seat. Once she's safely inside, I make my way around the car and slip into the driver's seat. Slamming the car in drive I peel out of the driveway and take off back to Fallyn's place.

"*Bellisima*, are you okay?"

She doesn't answer me. She just stares out the window.

"Fallyn, please talk to me. What happened? Where did they take you?"

Suddenly, she whips around to look at me. "Did you know?"

"Did I know what?"

"That my mother has been alive this entire time?"

"What?"

Slamming on the breaks, I pull over into an empty parking lot and turn to face her.

"*Bellisima*, I swear to you, if I knew anything or had any idea that your mother was alive, I would've told you. I know how much you miss her."

I watch her, waiting for a response, but she doesn't say a word. Instead, she bursts into uncontrollable tears. Undoing her seatbelt, I grab her and pull her into my lap, holding her against my chest.

"Fallyn, please talk to me."

Her body shakes from her sobs as she chokes out the words, "I killed her."

"You killed who? I don't understand?"

"Your father made me murder my own mother."

"That son of a bitch!"

"It was either her or you, me, and my father. I didn't want to do it, Emilio. She's my mom. But she begged me to do it so he wouldn't hurt us. I-I don't know how I'm going to get through this."

"*Bellisima*, you are my world, and I will do whatever it takes to help you get through this."

I hold her against me until her tears stop. She moves back into her seat and buckles up as I make short time of getting to the house. When I pull into the driveway, Chief Monroe comes rushing out the door. Jumping out of the driver's seat, I make my way around to the passenger side and help Fallyn out.

When she stands, her knees buckle but I quickly scoop her up into my arms and carry her inside. The chief grabs a blanket to cover her as I place her on the couch.

He drops to his knees next to her. "I'm so sorry, princess. I love you so much. I promise, I will do whatever it takes to make everything right."

She stares at him blankly as a tear streams down her cheek. "I love you too. I just want to sleep for now."

"Okay princess, get some rest. Me and Emilio will be in the kitchen if you need us."

He places a kiss on her cheek and we make our way into the kitchen. The conversation we're about to have may fuck up my relationship with her father, but he's going to give me some answers.

"Did you know that Lily was still alive?" I spit the question at him as soon as we're out of earshot of Fallyn.

His eyes widen before his head dips between his shoulders. "Yes."

"Excuse me?"

"I said yes. Yes, I know my wife is still alive."

I'm taken aback by his answer. Never in my life did I think he actually knew she was alive.

"Was."

"Was what?"

"She *was* still alive."

"What do you mean? What happened to her? How do you even know she is-was alive?"

"My father. He forced Fallyn to kill her. It was either her or us. Fallyn said Lily begged her to kill her to keep the three of us safe."

I watch Chief Monroe battle between two emotions, sadness and rage. "This is all my fault."

"What do you mean?"

He bows his head again. "I faked her death and put her in protective custody to keep her safe from your father… But he must… must've figured it out."

I press fingers to my temples, rubbing them in a circular motion while trying to process all of this. "Okay, let's start at the beginning… I need to know everything if you want my help to take my father down for good."

The chief grabs two beers from the fridge, popping the tops on them and handing me one before he takes a seat at the table.

He takes a deep breath, "So, before I became the chief of police, I got myself into some financial trouble. I was illegally gambling, and dug myself into a pretty deep hole. I was on the verge of losing any chance of being able to become police chief. That's when your father made me a deal I couldn't refuse at the time.

"He promised to pay off my debt and guaranteed I would be appointed the chief of police. I knew there was a catch, but I didn't care. It was either make a deal with the devil or lose everything I had worked for, I chose the devil. But as I stood there and took an oath to serve and protect my community, I couldn't go through with whatever your father had in mind."

He pauses, taking a long swig of his beer before continuing. "When I refused to do what he wanted me to, he threatened to torture and kill Lily and Fallyn. I was scared for them. I confided in Mayor Franklyn Sr. about what was going on. He said he could help keep them safe, but it would come with a price. He said he would help me fake Lily's death and keep Fallyn safe, if I promised her hand to Ethan."

I listen to him silently when really on the inside, I'm raging.

He sighs. "Once I realized your father had Franklyn Sr. in his pocket, it was too late."

I run my hands over my face, and then take a long drink of my beer. "Well… that sure explains a lot. Franklyn Sr. must've disclosed the location of Lily's safe house after Ethan died."

"He must have…" He chokes back a sob as his eyes start to fill with tears. "Now my wife is dead and when Fallyn finds out I've known all along, she's going to hate me."

"She won't hate you… but you need to tell her, and soon."

A voice comes from the doorway, startling both of us. "Tell me what?"

# Chapter 20

## Fallyn

I lean against the doorway to the kitchen, mainly because I need to the wall to hold me up. Emilio immediately comes to my side, hugging me tightly before releasing me and walking me to the table to sit down. My dad doesn't say anything, he just watches me like at any moment I might break.

My curiosity is peaked to know what he needs to tell me but at the same time, an uneasy feeling settles in the pit of my stomach. Something in his expression tells me I'm not going to like whatever it is.

Grabbing another beer from the fridge, he takes a deep breath as he makes his way over to the table. He grabs one of the chairs and pulls it up in front of me and takes a seat.

"Fallyn, you know how much I love you, right? That I would do anything in this world to keep you safe?"

"Yes, I know. I love you, too."

He closes his eyes and sighs as he takes my hands in his, giving them a light squeeze.

"There's something that I need to tell you… but you have to understand, I did what I had to do to keep you safe."

I sit in my chair, staring at him blankly when it hits me. "You knew mom was alive, didn't you?"

"Yes," he whispers. "We faked her death and put her in a safe house."

Sadness, confusion… anger rushes through me and I yank my hands back out of my father's hands as I jump to my feet.

"YOU KNEW?" I shout at him. "How could you keep something like this from me? How could you let me believe my mother was dead for almost three years!"

"Princess, it was to keep you safe! You have to believe me; I didn't have any other choice! It had to be believable so that Eli wouldn't suspect anything."

"Eli? Why would he want to kill mom?" I spin around to face Emilio, who's standing against the wall quietly. "Did you know?"

"No, I didn't know anything about this until just before you walked in here. If I had known, I would've told you."

I turn back to look at my father and he shakes his head in confirmation that Emilio is telling me the truth.

"Fallyn, just please sit back down and I will tell you everything."

I pace the kitchen, trying to reign in the emotions overpowering me. Finally, I take a seat and wave him on to explain. My father finishes off his beer before he begins.

He tells me everything; from the illegal gambling to making a deal with Eli Manzini. From becoming chief to making a deal with the Mayor and faking my mother's death. When he's finished, I just stare at him, not really sure how to react or what to say.

Tears unwillingly stream down my face and I get angry all over again. I don't say a word to my father as I stand and walk out of the room.

Both him and Emilio follow me into the living room as I'm gathering some of my things.

“Fallyn, please say something.”

“I can’t right now. I have to get out of here. Emilio, please take me to your place.”

He glances between me and my father before nodding.

Turning on my heel, I walk out the door to Emilio’s car without as much as a glance back to my father.

# Chapter 21

## Emilio

I stand in the kitchen as Fallyn's father tells her everything. All I want to do is hold her and comfort her, knowing she isn't going to take this news well. But I've known her long enough to know right now, it's better to stay back.

When her father finishes explaining everything, I'm half expecting her to explode, but she doesn't. Chief Monroe and I watch as Fallyn grabs a duffle bag of clothes and asks that I take her with me before walking out of the house.

I glance at the chief; he looks broken and sad. "It'll be okay, Chief. She just needs some time to process things. I'll keep her safe. I'll give you a call tomorrow and we can figure out exactly how we're going to take out my father."

"Thank you, Emilio."

"You're welcome. Have a good night." I briefly touch his shoulder before heading out the door to join Fallyn in the car.

I slide into the front seat as Fallyn stares out the window, silent tears streaming down her face. Starting the car, I pull out of the driveway and take off towards my place. Unsure what to say to comfort her, I just reach over and take her hand in mine.

For the first time since we left, she looks up at me, a deep sadness in her eyes that breaks my heart into a million pieces. I'm not sure how she's going to get through all of this but there is nothing in this world I won't do to help her. I lift her hand in mine, placing a kiss to the back of hers before laying our hands back in her lap. The corner of her mouth tips up in a small smile as we ride in silence the rest of the way to my place.

Fallyn drops her duffle bag on the floor inside the door and collapses onto the couch. Walking into the kitchen, I grab two glasses and pour two fingers of whiskey in both. I walk back out into the living room and take a seat next to Fallyn, handing her a glass.

"Whiskey," I answer her unspoken question.

"Thank you."

She tosses the glass back, downing the smooth liquid and places the glass on the table. Sitting back, she rests her head against the couch with her eyes closed. I want to ask if she's okay, but really, who would be okay with everything that has happened today?

"I hate this. I hate being angry with my father, but how can I forgive him after what he's done?"

I'm silent for a moment, waiting to see if she speaks again. "I know none of this makes any sense right now, that you're angry and hurt, but I believe he honestly thought he was doing the right thing."

She scoffs. "There's nothing to make sense of. He lied to me. He told me my mother was dead! I buried her three years ago, only to be kidnapped by your sick bastard of a father and forced to kill her myself or lose my own life and the lives of everyone I love." Her tears are flowing again and her breaths come out in puffs.

I turn, sitting on the edge of the couch as I pull her towards me and lay us both down. Wrapping my arms around her, I crush her to my chest and let her cry as long as she needs to.

Right now, I know there is nothing I can say or do to make things better for her. All I can do is be here and let her know that I'm not going anywhere.

# Chapter 22

## *Three Months Later*

### Emilio

I'm sitting in the chair across from my father at his desk as he eyes my speculatively. I do my best to keep my cool even though I want to bash his skull in myself from all the shit he's done to Fallyn. It's a constant battle for her to get through each day thinking she's responsible for her mother's death.

"You don't trust me, I get it. But I have the sheriff where you've always wanted to have him. Right in my pocket. I'm with his little princess, and there's nothing he won't do for me."

"How do I know I can believe you?"

"You can't afford not to." I shrug. "You don't have that little bitch of a Mayor to do all your dirty work for you anymore, and we all know you won't do it yourself. I'm your last option."

He taps his chin as he stares at me, still skeptical, but he knows, as well as I do, he doesn't have any other options.

"Fine. But if you betray me, I will kill you myself."

"I wouldn't expect anything less."

He leans in towards me across his desk. "I have a big shipment of drugs and weapons coming in from Cuba. There's one thing I want more than the drugs though, I want the head guy's fingers. He shorted me on the last shipment, cost me a hundred grand."

"That won't be a problem. When is this shipment coming in?"

"Tonight. Eleven o'clock, at the private shipping docks."

"Okay. I'll be there."

"Oh, I know you will, because I'm coming with you to make sure there's no funny business going on."

# Chapter 23

## Emilio

The blacked out SUV pulls up to the docks where a small shipping boat waits. On the outside, I keep cool and composed so my father doesn't suspect anything. Four guys from the ship come down the ramp as we slide out of the SUV and approach them.

"Eli. It's been too long."

"Matias, it's great to see you. Do you have my goods?"

"I do," he says, looking over at me. "Who is this?"

"My son Emilio."

"Ahh, so you're the little pussy your father was telling me about."

I narrow my eyes at him as he throws his head back and cackles. When he brings his head back up, I place the gun from my waist band between his eyes. He puts his hands up and begs me not to shoot him.

"Who's the pussy now?"

I make him sweat a few minutes before I lower my gun, placing it back in my waistband.

"You transfer my money?" he asks my father.

"Just did." My father turns his phone to show Matias the transaction.

"Good, then we're all set."

Matias turns and waves to his guys to unload the boat. The three men disappear back into the boat and emerge with pallets of drugs. I cough once to clear my throat, signaling to Chief Monroe to move in.

Within minutes, its pure chaos as the entire police department moves in on my father, Matias, and his men. Matias' guys begin firing at the police and I pull my gun, shooting back and hitting two of them while one of the officers takes out the other.

My father runs for the protection of the SUV and is met by Chief Monroe. The chief grabs my father, slamming his head into the side of the SUV, bloodying his face.

"That was for my daughter and my wife, you son of a bitch. Now you can rot in hell for the rest of your life."

A few of the deputies wrestle Matias to the ground, cuffing him and reading him his rights as they stuff him into the back of a police cruiser. I make my way towards where my father and Chief Monroe stand.

"You set me up, you little bastard," my father spits at me.

"I guess sometimes blood isn't thicker than water. Have a nice life rotting in prison for the rest of your life," I spit back as the Chief stuffs him into the back of one of his deputy's police cars.

"Thank you, Emilio."

"You're welcome."

# Chapter 24

## Fallyn

The television is on low in the background as I pace the floor of the living room at my father's place, waiting to hear any kind of news from him or Emilio. Glancing at the TV, a breaking news banner flashes on the screen and I grab the remote to turn up the volume.

"Breaking news, Eli Manzini, Italian mob boss, and suspect in connection with multiple murders and drug trafficking cases, has been arrested. Three people are dead after a raid at the riverside docks. One officer was shot and has been taken to a local hospital for medical attention but he is expected to make a full recovery," the newscaster reports.

Panic rises in me. Three dead? What if it was my dad? Or Emilio? Grabbing my phone, I call both of them but neither of them answers. Not able to wait any longer, I grab the keys to my SUV and head for the door just as Emilio comes bursting through it.

"Oh my god, Emilio! Are you okay?"

"I'm fine, I'm okay," he assures me, as I wrap my arms around him.

"What about my dad?"

"He's okay too."

"And your dad?"

"Your father had a deputy get a warrant for the house while we were at the docks. They found enough evidence to link him to every murder linked to drugs over the past two years. He's going to prison for the rest of his life and we'll never have to worry about him again."

"Thank god."

Standing on my tip toes, I place a kiss on Emilio's lips and he wraps his hands up in my hair as he kisses me back. The stress of everything we have been through slowly lifts from my shoulders and for the first time since we've gotten together, everything feels lighter.

Releasing him, I take his hand and lead him to the couch to sit and we watch everything play out on the TV as multiple news stations begin to cover the story of how the elusive Eli Manzini has been arrested.

I'm startled awake to the sound of the front door opening and then shutting. Both Emilio and I must've dozed off on the couch watching the news. I look towards the door to find my father placing his badge and gun on the table by the door. I jump to my feet and run to him, wrapping my arms tight around him as tears swell up in my eyes.

"I'm so sorry, Daddy."

"No princess, I'm the one that's sorry. I should've told you what was going on a long time ago."

"It's okay."

Both of us are silent as we stand there holding one another. Suddenly, there's a noise at the back door and both Emilio and my father draw their guns. Footsteps sound on the hardwood floors from the door in the back family room of the house. The person's shadow casts onto the wall as they come into view.

My breath catches in my throat, threatening to strangle me. “Mom?” I whisper. “Is it really you?”

“Yeah, honey, it’s me.”

“But… but I thought I killed you?”

“I had to make you believe you killed me. Eli’s guys needed to believe I was dead. As soon as I heard you all pull away, I ran from the house, and kept running until I found somewhere to hide. I was with a friend in a small dive bar watching the news when I saw Eli was arrested and I immediately came here. I’m so sorry you had to go through all this. It was never meant to turn out this way.”

I walk over to her, placing my hand on her cheek, still not completely sure she’s really here. She places her hand over mine.

“It’s really me, babygirl. I promise.”

“I love you,” I say through tears as I hug her like she might disappear at any minute.

My father makes his way over to us, wrapping us up in his arms as we stand there together, relieved that this nightmare is finally over. I look over at Emilio as he stands by the door watching us with a smile on his face.

*“Thank you,”* I mouth to him and he smiles.

Once I’m sure my mother isn’t going to disappear, I release her, walking over to Emilio. He wraps his arm around my shoulders pulling me into his side and kisses my hair.

“Fallyn?”

“Yes?”

“Now that this is all over and you finally have your mom back, there is something I’ve been wanting to ask you for a while now.”

Him and my father have a weird exchange with their eyes before he drops his arm from my shoulders and kneels in front of me, pulling a little red velvet box from his pocket.

“Fallyn Monroe, I have been in love with you for as long as I can remember. When you agreed to be my girl, I knew this was it; you were the one I wanted to spend forever with. As the days passed, I became even more sure. You are the most kind, caring, and compassionate person I have ever met.

“Over the past year, there have been times when I expected you to run away from me and never look back, but you didn’t. You stuck by my side and loved me, despite my flaws and mishaps. I love you with all my heart, and there is no one in the universe I would ever want to spend my life with more than I do with you. So, will you do me the greatest honor of being my wife?”

The tears come again as I do my best to blink them away. I glance at my father who gives me a smile and shrugs before I turn back to Emilio.

“YES! Yes, I will marry you.”

# Acknowledgments

**Katy McCain –** Who knew a simple request for a specific model would turn into an amazing friendship. Thank you for agreeing to be my Fallyn. <3 Love you to the moon and back!

**Kyle English –** You are amazing. <3 I find it hard to put into words how much you mean to me, but it's a lot. Thank you for gracing so many of my covers already and the many yet to come.

**Melissa Taegel-Parnell –** Thank you for being such a great friend and assistant. Your continued support means the world to me and I can't thank you enough for coming on this journey with me.

**My beta babes: Tanya Turner, Jamie Margulis Speck, R.S. James, & Brittney Lathan –** Thank you for taking the time out of your schedules to read my words and offer feedback to make these stories better. I appreciate you all more than I could ever put into words. <3

**Jean Maureen Woodfin –** Thank you for your amazing artistry when it comes to photography. The beauty you capture from behind the lens helps to bring my characters to life. I am in awe and thankful for what you do. <3

# Also by Cheri Marie

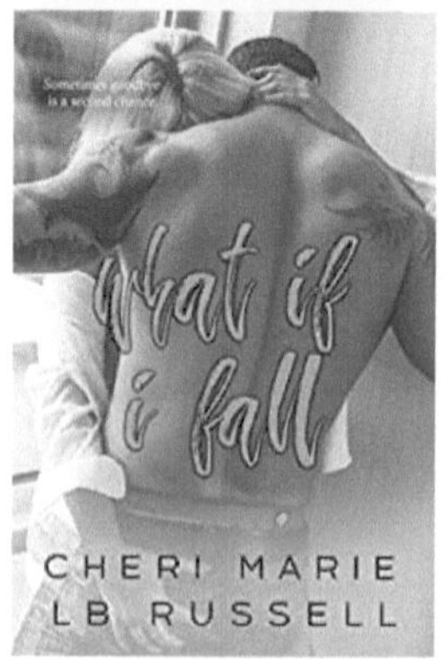

# About the Author

Cheri Marie is a self-published author. She resides in sunny Southwest Florida with family and a house full of animals. Her first book, Hearts Aligned, published in 2016 and it's been a wild ride since.

On her free time you can find her writing poetry, spending time with friends, or taking long drives with the radio turned all the way up singing at the top of her lungs.

www.ingramcontent.com/pod-product-compliance
Ingram Content Group UK Ltd.
Pitfield, Milton Keynes, MK11 3LW, UK
UKHW041641190726
13854UKWH00006B/2627